Maxwell Moose's Mountain Monster

by Barbara deRubertis • illustrated by R.W. Alley

THE KANE PRESS / NEW YORK

Alpha Betty's Class

Alexander Anteater

Bobby Baboon

Corky Cub

Dilly Dog

Eddie Elephant

Frances Frog

Gertie Gorilla

Hanna Hippo

Lana Llama

Izzy Impala

Jeremy Jackrabbit

Kylie Kangaroo

Maxwell Moose

STAR of the BOOK

Library of Congress Cataloging-in-Publication Data

deRubertis, Barbara.
Maxwell Moose's mountain monster / by Barbara deRubertis ; illustrated by R.W. Alley.
p. cm. — (Animal antics A to Z)
Summary: Maxwell Moose scares his friends with his spooky stories when they are camping out.
ISBN 978-1-57565-334-1 (library binding : alk. paper) — ISBN 978-1-57565-325-9 (pbk. : alk. paper)
[1. Moose—Fiction. 2. Camping—Fiction. 3. Storytelling—Fiction. 4. Alphabet.]
I. Alley, R. W. (Robert W.), ill. II. Title.
PZ7.D4475Max 2011
[E]—dc22   2010021824

1 3 5 7 9 10 8 6 4 2

First published in the United States of America in 2011 by Kane Press, Inc.
Printed in the United States of America
WOZ0111

Series Editor: Juliana Hanford
Book Design: Edward Miller

Animal Antics A to Z is a registered trademark of Kane Press, Inc.

www.kanepress.com

Maxwell Moose moved closer to the campfire. This was his last camping trip of the summer.

On Monday morning he would be going back to Alpha Betty's school.

5

Maxwell loved camping in the mountains.
He loved smoky campfires. He loved telling stories.

And he especially loved camping with his chums
Mitzi Mouse and Murphy Muskrat.

"Tell us a spooky story, Maxwell!" said Mitzi.
"About the Mountain Monster!" said Murphy.

Maxwell's Mountain Monster stories were their
favorite part of camping out.

"Sure!" Maxwell smiled. "After we make s'mores!"

"Yum, yum, yummy! S'mores for our tummies!"
sang Mitzi Mouse and Murphy Muskrat.

Maxwell got out marshmallows, graham
crackers, and chocolate bars.

He mashed the marshmallows onto some twigs.
"Hold these over the campfire," Maxwell said.

Mitzi's marshmallow smoked and bubbled.
Murphy's marshmallow melted and oozed.

Maxwell slid the marshmallows onto the
melting chocolate and graham crackers.
And the three chums munched on their s'mores.

"Mmm," they hummed. "Messy . . . but amazing!"

A million stars twinkled.
The moon was smiling down.
It was a magical moment.

The campfire dimmed. "Time for some spooky stories!" said Maxwell.

"Oh, yes!" said Mitzi and Murphy.
"Tell us about the Mountain Monster!"

Maxwell began. "Once upon a time, there was
a Mountain Monster living right here. . . ."

"He was humongous," said Maxwell.
"He had massive muscles. He was smelly and mean.
But the scariest thing about him was his SCREAM."

Maxwell made a terrible monster moan.

HOOOOO HOOOOO

Mitzi and Murphy trembled. "He's just a make-believe monster," they murmured to each other.

But they moved closer to Maxwell Moose.

Maxwell continued. "One night the Mountain
Monster woke up HUNGRY!

He marched down the mountain like a zombie.
He was looking for yummy munchies,
like worms and mushrooms . . .
and fingers and toes!"

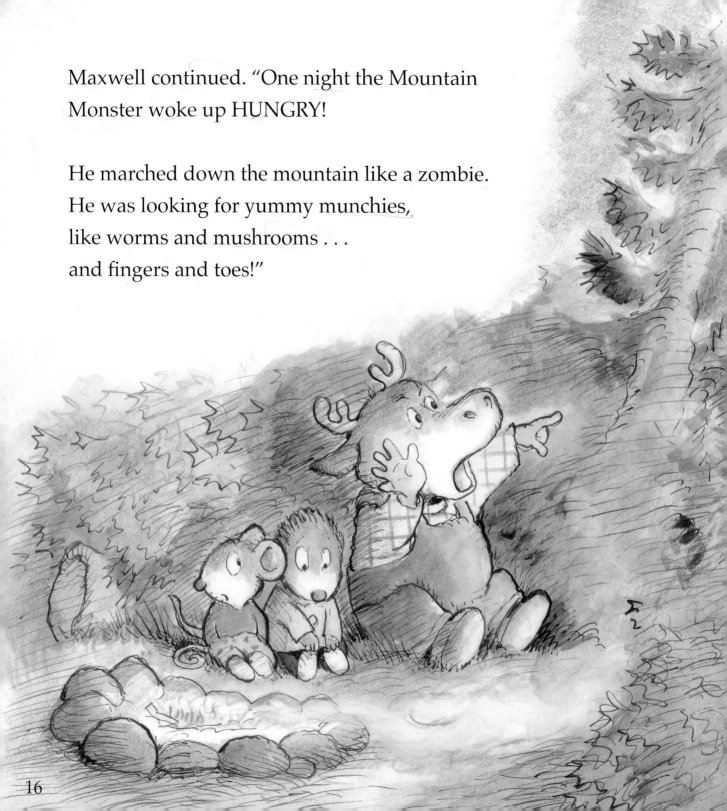

Mitzi pushed her fingers into her pockets.
Murphy pulled his coat down over his toes.

The both moved even closer to Maxwell.

17

"The Mountain Monster saw a campfire,"
Maxwell said in a booming voice.

"And he smelled s'mores. . . .
'Mmm,' said the monster, 'I like s'mores.
But I LOVE little MOUSE FINGERS and
little MUSKRAT TOES!'"

Mitzi and Murphy both screamed.
"The Mountain Monster is imaginary!
He's imaginary! Isn't he, Maxwell?"

Suddenly they heard a terrible moan.

HOOOO

Maxwell jumped. He looked frightened.
"That moan wasn't from me," he whispered.

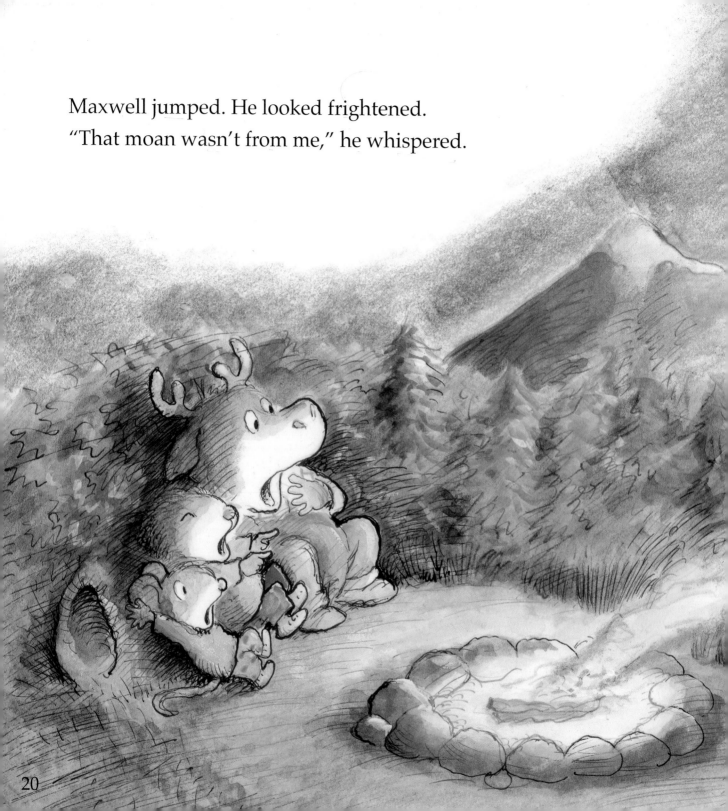

"It came from the mountain!" cried Mitzi.

"It came from the MONSTER!"
cried Murphy.

A rumbling, bumbling shape was moving toward them.

Mitzi screamed, "We're doomed!"
Murphy screamed, "We're monster food!"

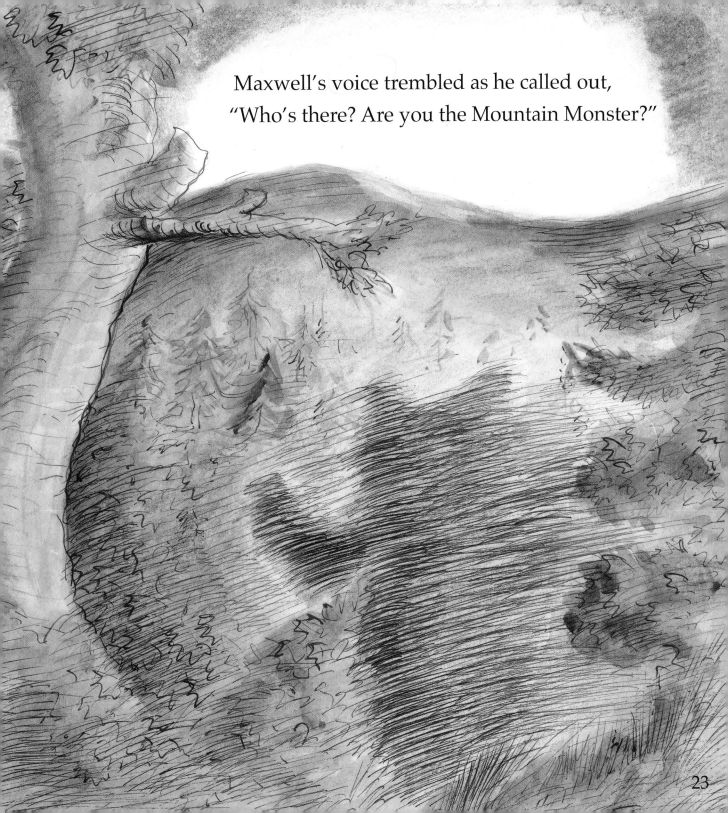

Maxwell's voice trembled as he called out,
"Who's there? Are you the Mountain Monster?"

A voice called back, "Maxwell, calm down!
It's ME! Your MOTHER!"

"Oh, MAMA!" cried Maxwell.

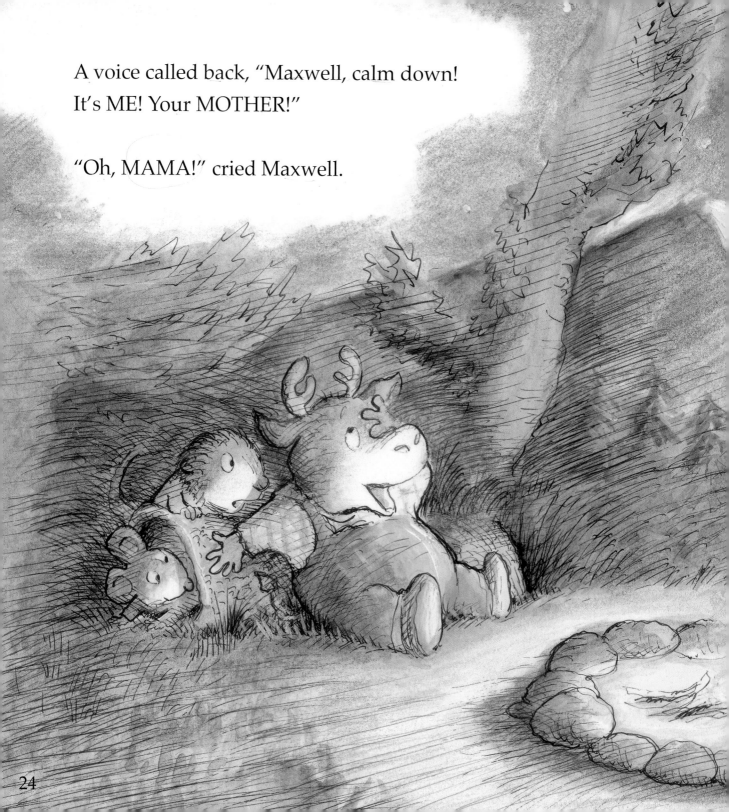

Mama Moose moved into the light of the campfire.

"It's mighty chilly," she said. "So I've come with some mittens and earmuffs for you."

Mama Moose put her arms around Maxwell,
Mitzi, and Murphy.

"Let's put another log on the campfire," she said.
"I also brought you some oatmeal muffins
and mushroom soup. You need more than
just s'mores to eat!"

Soon their tummies were warm and full,
and their eyes were sleepy.

Mama Moose said, "I'm going home now,
Maxwell. So please don't tell any more stories
about that imaginary Mountain Monster!"

Maxwell Moose called out, "Wait, Mama!
What if the Mountain Monster IS real?
What if he DOES come?"

"Just make him s'mores, Maxwell," she told him.
"He actually likes them MUCH better than
mouse fingers or muskrat toes . . .
or MOOSE TAILS!"

29

Maxwell, Mitzi, and Murphy all laughed.
"See you in the morning!" Maxwell called out
to Mama.

Then he whispered to Mitzi and Murphy,
"After we make more s'mores for breakfast!"

The three chums put out their campfire for the night.

And within minutes, the only sound on the mountain was the sound of snoring.

STAR OF THE BOOK: THE MOOSE

FUN FACTS

- **Home:** Moose live in the northern parts of North America, Europe, and Asia.
- **Family:** The moose is the largest member of the deer family.
- **Antlers:** Male moose have broad, flat antlers that can grow to be 6 feet wide! They shed their antlers in the fall and grow new ones in the spring.
- **Size:** An adult male moose can be 7 feet tall and weigh as much as 1,800 pounds!
- **Did You Know?** Moose are excellent swimmers. Some have swum across lakes that are many miles wide!

LOOK BACK

Learning to identify letter sounds (phonemes) at the beginning, middle, and end of words is called "phonemic awareness."

- The word *moose* <u>begins</u> with the *m* sound. Listen to the words on page 11 being read again. When you hear a word that <u>begins</u> with the *m* sound, say "Mmm!"
- The word *tummy* has the *m* sound in the <u>middle</u>. Listen to the words on page 22 being read again. When you hear words that have the *m* sound in the middle, say "Yummy!"
- **Challenge:** The word *scream* <u>ends</u> with the *m* sound. Can you think of 2 words that rhyme with *scream*?

TRY THIS!

***Mmm, Mmm*, Where Is the *Mmm* Sound?**

- Write a large *m* on a piece of paper. Now sit on a chair and listen carefully as each word in the word bank is read aloud slowly.
- If the word <u>begins</u> with the *m* sound, hold the *m* above your head!
- If the word has the *m* sound in the <u>middle</u>, hold the *m* in front of your tummy!
- If the word <u>ends</u> with the *m* sound, hold the *m* above your feet!

| moose earmuffs warm rumbling dream mitten room camping mother storm tremble mouse |

FOR MORE ACTIVITIES, go to Maxwell Moose's website: www.kanepress.com/AnimalAntics/MaxwellMoose.html You'll also find a recipe for Maxwell Moose's Oven-Baked S'mores!